Places in My Community

Learning at Pre-K

Celeste Bishop

illustrated by
Aurora Aguilera

PowerKiDS press.

New York

Published in 2017 by The Rosen Publishing Group, Inc.
29 East 21st Street, New York, NY 10010

First Edition

Managing Editor: Nathalie Beullens-Maoui
Editor: Theresa Morlock
Book Design: Mickey Harmon
Illustrator: Aurora Aguilera

Cataloging-in-Publication Data

Names: Bishop, Celeste.
Title: Learning at Pre-K / Celeste Bishop.
Description: New York : PowerKids Press, 2017. | Series: Places in my community | Includes index.
Identifiers: ISBN 9781499427745 (pbk.) | ISBN 9781499430141 (library bound) | ISBN 9781508152903 (6 pack)
Subjects: LCSH: Education, Preschool—Juvenile literature. | Preschool children—Juvenile literature.
Classification: LCC LB1140.2 B57 2017 | DDC 372.21—dc23

Manufactured in the United States of America

CPSIA Compliance Information: Batch #BW17PK: For Further Information contact Rosen Publishing, New York, New York at 1-800-237-9932

Contents

There's a school in my community.

I'm in Pre-K this year.

6

Pre-K is the year
of school before
kindergarten.

7

All my friends are in my class.

I make new friends, too.

10

My teacher reads us stories. I like the stories about animals.

11

My class does arts and crafts, too.

I like to draw.

We go outside every day.

14

There's a playground at my school.

I like to climb on the monkey bars!

There's also a slide. Wee!

I get tired from playing.
It's time to take a nap.

18

When naptime is over,
it's time for a snack.

The cereal is my favorite.

Soon, it's time to go home.
My dad picks me up. I'll be
back tomorrow!

Words to Know

cereal

monkey bars

slide

Index

24